All About Tigger

DEAN

This edition first published in Great Britain in 2012
by Dean, an imprint of Egmont UK Limited
The Yellow Building, 1 Nicholas Road, London W11 4AN
© 2019 Disney Enterprises, Inc
Based on the Winnie-the-Pooh works by A. A. Milne and E. H. Shepard
Illustrations by Andrew Grey
Text by Jude Exley

ISBN 978 0 6035 6666 0
51659/003
Printed in Great Britain

Meet Tigger

Here is Tigger, ready to be introduced to you. He may be bouncing rather a lot, but that is because he is very excited to meet you. As you may know, Tigger is a very bouncy animal and a very

friendly Tigger.

In this book you will learn about the strange animal called Tigger, including what he really likes to eat for breakfast. And you can listen to a story about Tigger – a bouncy story. Because Tigger does rather a lot of that . . .

In which we read about Tigger

One night Pooh woke up suddenly when he thought he heard somebody trying to get into his honey cupboard. He got out of bed, but there was no one there. There was just a strange noise. There are lots of noises in the Forest, but this was different. It wasn't a growl

or a purr,

or a squeak,

or a neigh,

like Piglet or Eeyore might make, it was a

"Worraworraworraworraworra".

Pooh decided to ask the strange animal making that noise not to do it again. He opened his front door and said "hello".

The strange animal introduced himself as Tigger. Pooh had never seen a Tigger before, but he was very pleased to hear that he was a friend of Christopher Robin's and invited him in.

"Do Tiggers like honey?" asked Pooh.

"Tiggers like everything," said Tigger, happily.

And they both went to sleep.

The next morning, Pooh woke up to see Tigger looking at himself in the mirror. "I thought I was the only one," said Tigger, "but I've just met someone like me!"

Then suddenly Tigger jumped at Pooh's tablecloth and with a loud

"Worraworraworraworra",

he pulled it off the table and rolled across the room with it.

"Did I win?" he asked, cheerfully.

"That's my tablecloth," replied Pooh, putting the cloth and two pots of honey on the table.

They both sat down to breakfast and Tigger helped himself to a large mouthful of honey, making exploring movements with his tongue . . .

and "what-is-this noises"? . . .
and then he said:

"Tiggers don't like honey."

"I thought they liked everything," said Pooh, trying to sound disappointed, but actually feeling very pleased – particularly when Tigger said that they liked everything **except** honey.

So Pooh took Tigger to Piglet's house. Piglet had
never seen a Tigger before and he was a little bit scared.
But Pooh explained that Tigger would like some
haycorns for breakfast and Piglet said, "Help yourself".

When Tigger had a mouthful of haycorns, he said

"Ee-ers o i a-ors"
and then
"skoos ee",

before saying firmly: "Tiggers don't like haycorns."

Piglet was rather
glad and asked if
he liked thistles
instead, and
Tigger said
that was what
he liked best.

Then the three of them went to the part of the Forest where Eeyore lived. Eeyore was a little unsure of Tigger at first, and asked what he was and when he was going. But when Pooh explained that he was a friend of Christopher Robin's who wanted some thistles for breakfast, Eeyore showed him to a very thistly looking patch of thistles.

Tigger wasn't sure that these really were the thistles that Tiggers like best, but he took a large, crunchy mouthful.

"Ow! Hot!" said Tigger, putting his paw in his mouth and shaking his head to get the prickles out.

Eeyore thought that Tigger had eaten a bee, but Tigger, running round in circles with his tongue hanging out, explained that Tiggers don't like thistles.

Pooh was very confused. Tiggers didn't like honey, haycorns or thistles. Maybe Christopher Robin could help? So they went to find Christopher Robin, with Tigger bouncing in front of them, turning round every now and then to check that this was the right way.

Soon Tigger saw Christopher Robin, and rushed up to him.

"Oh, there you are, Tigger!" said Christopher Robin.

Pooh asked Christopher Robin what Tiggers like to eat for breakfast, but he didn't know either. He thought Kanga would be able to help. So they all went to Kanga's house.

Pooh was very pleased to find some **condensed milk** in her cupboard. But Tigger put his nose into this and his paw into that, and he still couldn't find anything that Tiggers like.

Then he saw Kanga trying to give Roo his
Strengthening Medicine. Roo was trying his best
not to have it, when Tigger suddenly put out his tongue
and the Extract of Malt medicine went straight into
Tigger's mouth.

"Tigger, dear!" said Kanga.

"He's taken my medicine!" sang Roo happily.

Then Tigger closed his eyes, moved his tongue round
and round, and with a happy smile on his face said, "So,
that's what Tiggers like!"

Everyone was very happy to know finally what Tiggers like. And from then on, it was decided that Tigger would live at Kanga's house, so he could eat Extract of Malt for breakfast, dinner and tea. And sometimes as Strengthening Medicine, too.

A few days later, Kanga was beginning to realise that there were times when a bouncy animal like Tigger shouldn't be in the house. So she sent Tigger and Roo out to have a nice long morning in the Forest, not getting into mischief.

Tigger was telling Roo about all the things Tiggers can do. Roo was very excited to learn that climbing trees is what Tiggers do best.

So Roo sat on Tigger's back and Tigger began to climb a very tall tree. It was going well, until . . .

Snap! . . .

the branch he was standing on broke . . . and Tigger had to climb quickly on to the one above it. Roo was having lots of fun and he couldn't wait to go higher, but Tigger told him that he didn't want to go higher and his tail got in the way if he tried to climb down.

Just then, Pooh and Piglet came along.

"Hallo, Roo," called Piglet. "What are you doing?"

"We can't get down!" cried Roo. "Isn't it fun? Tigger and I are living in a tree, just like Owl."

Pooh and Piglet didn't know how to get them down either. Luckily, Christopher Robin came strolling along, and decided that he would take off his tunic, so they could hold it out under the tree for Roo and Tigger to jump into.

Roo was wildly excited, and he jumped straight into the tunic, bouncing back up into the air when he landed, and saying "Oo, lovely!" for a while.

Tigger was less sure. He was holding on to the branch nervously, until suddenly, with a crash and a tearing noise, Tigger flew past the tree and landed in a heap with everyone on the ground. They all picked themselves up and Tigger bounced happily away with little Roo.

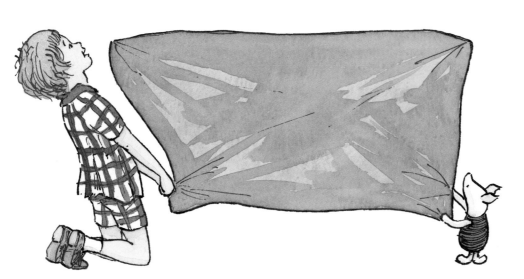

After a while, some of the animals in the Forest began to get annoyed by Tigger's bounciness.

One sunny day, Rabbit was talking to Pooh and Piglet about teaching Tigger a lesson. Piglet agreed that however much you liked Tigger, it was a very good idea to think of a way of unbouncing him. But he wasn't sure how they should do it. And Pooh was humming to himself, so it was left to Rabbit to come up with an idea.

Rabbit decided that they would take Tigger exploring to the North Pole and lose him there, so that by the time he found his way home, he would be a very different Tigger altogether. Pooh was glad that they were going to the North Pole, as Tigger would see the sign that said Pooh found it and then he would know what sort of bear he was.

The next morning, it was cold and misty. Piglet
was worried about how miserable it would be for
Tigger to be lost on a day like this. But Rabbit thought it
was the perfect weather, as when Tigger bounced out of
sight, they could hide and he wouldn't be able to
see them.

"Not never?" said Piglet, worriedly.
"Well, not until we find him again," said Rabbit.

At Kanga's house, Tigger and Roo were very pleased to see their friends and very excited at the thought of an adventure. But Rabbit didn't think Tigger's good friend Roo should come along.

"He was coughing earlier," he said to Kanga.

"It was just a biscuit cough," said Roo.

"Oh, Roo dear," said Kanga. "You can go another day." And it was decided that he would stay at home.

So, off they went. Pooh, Rabbit and Piglet walked together, with Tigger running around them in circles, squares, and when the bushes got prickly, up and down in front of them. He kept bouncing into Rabbit and then disappearing in the mist.

Rabbit decided that now was the right time, and he jumped into a gap beside the path and Pooh and Piglet followed him.

The Forest was silent. Then they heard Tigger say:

"hello?"

They all waited silently until they heard him wander off. Piglet felt very brave. When they were sure he had left, and they were all beginning to get a bit scared in the dark gap, they hurried off, with Rabbit leading the way home.

"Why are we going this way?" asked Pooh.

"I thought we went right," said Piglet, nervously.

But Rabbit was sure he knew the way, and half an hour later, he kept saying,

"here we are," and
"no, we're not."

And then,

"it's lucky I know the Forest
so well, or we might get lost."

Tigger waited for the others to catch him up, but when he got tired of waiting, he went home. Kanga was waiting for him with his Strengthening Medicine.

Just as they finished dinner, Christopher Robin arrived. He soon realised that Pooh, Piglet and Rabbit were lost in the Forest.

"Tiggers never get lost," whispered Tigger to Roo.

Christopher Robin asked Tigger to help him find them and off they went.

Rabbit, Pooh and Piglet were having a rest in a sand pit that they seemed to keep ending up in. Pooh was sure that his honey pots were calling him, but he couldn't hear them because Rabbit kept talking. So Pooh persuaded Rabbit to set off again by himself. Rabbit walked into the mist, and after twenty minutes, Pooh and Piglet walked off together.

Just when Pooh and Piglet began to know where they were, out of the mist came Christopher Robin.

"Oh, there you are," he said carelessly, trying to pretend he wasn't worried. "Tigger will find Rabbit. He's sort of looking for you all."

"We are just going home for a little something," said Pooh, and Christopher Robin decided to go home with them.

Meanwhile, Tigger was bouncing around the Forest, making loud yapping noises, looking for Rabbit.

At last, a very small and sorry Rabbit heard him. And he rushed to the noise to discover that it was a Friendly Tigger, who bounced in just the way a Tigger **should** bounce.

"Oh, Tigger, I am very glad to see you," he cried happily. And off they went home together.

Facts about Tigger

He came to the Forest late one night.
Pooh had never seen a Tigger before, and Tigger didn't
know what he liked, but they were both friends with
Christopher Robin.

He lives with Kanga and Roo in a different part
of the Forest to Pooh. There is a very good reason why he
lives with them, which will soon become clear.

He likes Extract of Malt -
Roo's Strengthening Medicine.
He has it for breakfast, dinner
and tea. That's why he lives at
Kanga's house!

He doesn't climb trees. Tigger thought that he did, but when he started to climb, he realised his tail got in the way and needed help to get back down.

 He is very bouncy.
So bouncy in fact, that he bounced Eeyore into the river, and Pooh thought that he was Piglet's stick in a game of Poohsticks.

 He never gets lost. He bounces and runs round in circles, squares and up and down, but Tigger never gets lost. They just don't, as Rabbit found out.

 He is a Friendly Tigger.
He is great friends with little
Roo who he could play with
all day. And when Rabbit
is lost in the Forest, Tigger
goes to find him.

He makes lots of unusual noises. When Tigger arrived
at Pooh's house, he said "Worraworraworraworraworra"
and he coughed "Grr-oppp-ptschschschz" when Eeyore
bounced into the river.

He is the only Tigger.
Well, he thinks he is, and is
very surprised when he finds
somebody just like him in
the mirror.

A Poem about Tigger

He came to the Forest late one night,
The noise was enough to give Pooh a fright.
"Worraworraworra," he said,
And Pooh got out of bed,
To find a Bouncy Tigger ahead.

Tigger now lives with Kanga and Roo,
Eating enough Medicine for two!
Never was an animal bouncier than he,
(Except when he was stuck up a tree.)

A Friendlier Tigger there never will be!